England's Darkness

SUN VISION
PRESS

England's Darkness

by Stephen Barber

ISBN 978-0-9857625-3-7

Published 2013 by Sun Vision Press

England's Darkness

The North Will Rise Again

Mercy's Eyes

Liberation's Ashes

England's Darkness

One Execration, Two Lamentations

England's Darkness

STEPHEN BARBER

All that now remains of England, are these documents, these fragments.

The first document was scoured from a palatial but burnt-out and erased global archive of 'destroyed lands', in the city of Linz.

The second document was located among the ground-down ruins of the Queen's Hotel, Leeds.

The third document was found placed, as though as an act of secrecy, into a rivet-split panel on the deck of a decommissioned and rust-fused oil-tanker in a frozen Riga dry-dock, its writer having disappeared without trace.

The fourth document was unearthed – along with a map (drawn on the rear side of a photograph showing a meeting of two dictators), from which almost all charcoal-inscribed traces and lines had seeped away – from a tin box buried deep under the soil, beside the site of T.E. Lawrence's cottage, Clouds Hills, in Dorset.

The final document was discovered, in the form of two salt-preserved shreds of human skin, fused-together and eroded to the point of near-illegibility, buried among stones under Hardraw Scar waterfall, and accidentally uncovered by the action of the water.

The North Will Rise Again

1

A bad era came down on England... Soon, after a few years of civil warfare, England was transformed into a destroyed land, and what remained of its memory – nothing at all, beyond a few fragments – was deposited in the archive of destroyed lands, in the city of Linz, a resilient global site for the perpetual preservation of all that survived, of lands that had fallen.

That land brought down its own destruction, as though compelled, as with a beast that cannot resist its set-down poison, knowing that it will kill it. Following England's long-foretold economic collapse, every other disintegration followed fast behind: first, and as though in unstoppable ecstasy, the collapse of all digital infrastructures, networks, transmissions, storage systems, together with the rendering obsolete of all systems of digital communication, telepresence and computing, both virtual and actual. Since the transferral of all of England's knowledge to those systems had only just been achieved – with the now-anachronistic media that had previously stored that knowledge all comprehensively erased, wiped and obliterated – that land became one of oblivion, with its knowledge, visions and sensations now instilled solely in the immediate corporeal presence and eyes of its inhabitants, at the exact moment that all knowledge, vision and sensation had been negated, blinded and numbed, within those bodies and those eyes.

The final lapsing of fossil-fuel reserves, especially oil and benzine, followed on near-simultaneously from the collapse of England's digital infrastructures, as though an unseen conflagration had incinerated those data-networks, and combusted the medium of conflagration along with its target. All that remained were immense reservoirs of petroleum, in reinforced tanks underneath the financial and corporate heart of London, located there to enable the resistance or flight of its governmental, administrative, military and corporate elites, in case of emergency, but inadvertently allowing, too – for any maleficent presence that chose to inflict such a fate – the instantaneous razing by fire of that city's heart.

Following the extinguishment of digital and fossil-based resources, England plummeted fast, as though its vertiginous fall impelled wildly flailing hands in descent to tear apart what remained, of the glory of that land. The cities had already fallen apart, and what had resisted, was shredded by those hands. The passion, so intense, for consumer culture – incandescent, full of longing, always touched by death – was brutally voided, so that England's great retail parks, multi-storey shopping malls, out-of-town retail centres, all became abandoned, as though all meaning had drained from them, like blood. Almost simultaneously, England's great business parks, its centres of excellence and innovation, and its technology hubs, also suffered neglect, so that their illuminated frontages, facades, image-screens and monocultural insignia all cracked and became cloven. The last tourists – those from Albania, now Europe's richest land – surveyed that disintegration, and laughed cruelly.

In that time, the people of England wrote nothing and said little. In their humiliation, they stood in compact groups under burnt-out street-lights, ashen, and looked out at their once-vibrant buildings and towers, as though in shame. Occasionally, someone would produce a concertina, accordion or harmonium, and with that accompaniment, sing a melancholy song. All food production and supply became impaired, and hunger came down, and anger.

England's governmental, administrative, corporate and military elites assessed the situation urgently. Two solutions presented themselves. Firstly, a strategic retrenching was essential, focused around England's South: its heart, and the site of its power for many centuries. With the erasure or extreme dilapidation of England's infrastructures, and the reduction to starvation-inducing conditions of its food resources, all means of survival needed to be concentrated in the South. No sentimentality could be shown: the North must become a wasteland, its now-extraneous inhabitants driven to depopulation or into exile, across the seas – north-eastwards, to Scandinavia, or westwards, to Ireland – or else rendered into subjugation, to generate essential resources for the South. Within the newly created wasteland of the North, a few cities would be allowed to subsist – those that, in previous centuries, had provided vast resources of steel, wool, and ingenious instruments of mechanical technology, as though, in their interim existence as financial hubs or sites of luxurious department-stores, those cities had solely dreamed aberrant dreams, of their coming industrial reactivation – through their transformation into new hells of toxic chemical mass-production, populated by the enslaved, whose lethal and intensive subjugation would facilitate both their own rapid human culling, and also engender much-needed consumer products to console the South, for England's fall. Those toxic subjugation-zone cities would no longer be known by their former names, such as Leeds, Bradford, Sheffield, Manchester, Middlesbrough; they would be rapidly butcher's knife-skinned of those names, to evoke instead the immense toxic pollution they would now be required to disgorge across the North, as the model-cities of Mutagen, Aluminium, Sulphuric-Acid, Magnox, Toxica. Secondly, the suppression and eventual extermination of England's North would demand vast conscript armies; mandatory incorporation within those forces would immediately engulf and diffuse the anger of populations now dispossessed of their iPhones and ultra-high-definition image-screens.

Soon, those immense conscript forces had been formed, and a map drawn up — the work of a senior bureaucrat, pen-hand hovering seismically, as two of his eager assistants took turns to fellate him — delineating the borderline division between the reduced terrain of England to be retained and secured, in the expectation of its imminent return to glory, and the wasteland-zones of the North, to be violently wrung and emptied. The first work of those conscript forces was to locate and exterminate all ecologists — of all dark, optimistic or intermediate factions — immediately and instantaneously, without discussion or hesitation, each shot in the base of the neck; a moment later, elimination camps had been established, to pacify the unruly elements of the North. The remaining population, after being graded according to criteria of servility and complicity, were assigned to work in the chemical plants, or, once each factory had reached its human saturation point – bursting with already-contaminated flesh – simply left to their own devices, in the expectation that they would find just causes, in their growing hunger and subjugation, to exterminate one another. The governmental forces then occupied and fortified each of the North's great cities, basing themselves in the open-plan suites and hot-desking offices of abandoned business parks and technology hubs, or in the chandeliered ballrooms of once-luxurious railway hotels, avoiding the urban peripheries, where the reactivation of toxic chemical industries became concentrated.

In the plan for the all-out subjugation of England's North, and its eventual evacuation and scorched-earth depopulation, Scotland, Wales and Cornwall were utterly disregarded, displaced into oblivion beyond the emergency concerns and future vision of England's governmental, administrative, corporate and military elites, and left to self-autonomy. But the North needed to be obliterated from the face of England, as though it provoked a memory-trace intimation of danger, in the near-voided sensorium of those elites. That trace soon proliferated, and began cascading into obsession. More conscript forces were ordered to head North, in phalanxes, each one hundred strong.

Soon, the chemical zonal cities of the North expelled concentrated toxic residues from many thousands of colossal aluminium chimneys arranged around the urban peripheries, generating virulent hallucinations of anger in the inhabitants of the North not already pacified in elimination camps, brutally subjugated by the conscript phalanxes, or thronging ports to gain a desperate exile to mainland Europe via long-obsolete trawlers or tankers so calamitously rusted-away that they were near-certain to sink down into the cold depths of the Northern seas. The governmental forces established themselves securely in their new centres of operation, in luxurious hotel ballrooms and business-park boardrooms, certain the subjugation-campaign would not last long, and fully implemented their slave state, overseen by conscript armies which incessantly traversed the expanses of the North, executing capricious acts of massacre, sexual abuse and limitless detention. But the future-oriented vision of the governmental, administrative, military and corporate elites of the South, in assassinating all ecological activists, thereby foreclosing potential resistance to the wastelanding and depopulation strategy for the North and its cities, neglected the presence of aberrant elements, lost in the cracks of those cities.

After two years of hard starvation-winters and punitive subjugation in the North, the first manifestations of resistance arose. Under darkness, figures huddled together in cellars, saliva rolling down their chins and ferocity in their voices, and began to make plans. The first Northern rebel brigades emerged: each of them named after the now near-forgotten punk-rock idols of the North, forty years or more after their moment of glory, and in many cases commanded either by those aged and gnarled figures, or by their children or grandchildren, in an immense lineage of refusal and nihilistic rage. Soon, in a rush of exhilaration, they were fully-armed: governmental conscripts were discovered dispossessed of their weapons, along with their heads, sexual organs and boots, in the tracts of dirt that surrounded their barracks, often positioned in close proximity to elimination camps or toxic-chemical plants to facilitate optimum enslavement of their occupants. The uprising took the South's governmental, administrative, military and corporate forces by surprise: complicity transformed itself into negation in the flash of an eye, and thousands of rebels began to make alliances across the North's wastelands.

Almost immediately, those alliances turned haywire, collapsing into vitriol, and the initial elation of the rebel brigades cracked into internecine disputes, over territories, affiliations, names and insignia. The rebel brigades began to massacre one another. During that same era, the Northern cities also became consumed by secondary disputes between their young inhabitants: factional gangwarfare combat over ownership rights to the eroded and multi-graffitied facades of abandoned business-towers, stockpiles of obsolete iPhones and other monoculture-debris of all kinds, as though those residues had acquired a mutating and lethal new power of seduction in their utter obsolescence. As the Northern cities rapidly disintegrated into terminal ruination, they formed the starvation-hit arenas for those split-lipped, throat-slicing gangs, mostly headed by contempt-impelled fourteen-year-old girls with dreams of implosion in their shock-haired heads. The rebel brigades disregarded those gangs and left them alone to their massacre games, aware that, if those brigades were wiped-out through their own in-fighting, or in their eventual direct confrontations with the conscript armies, it would fall solely to those gangs to liberate the North.

Finally, one rebel brigade subsumed all the others, and called a covert meeting, in the dead of a night of storms, at the former Assembly Rooms in the city of Leeds, its now-dark auditorium having served as a pornographic cinema for several decades, the lush seating still intact, hardened into permanent endurance with multiple layers of semen and encrusted dust, and the barely-visible projection-screen lacerated by shattering bottles hurled during the cacophonic furore of a final all-night projection of Japanese sex-massacre films, before that auditorium had been shut-down for over thirty years. The rebels sprawled over the seats, as though they had arrived for the next screening, but had then been frozen for decades in film-time. That pre-eminent brigade had no leader; the meeting was driven by all-engulfing fury, and the desire, above all, to erase all traces of England and its conception, cast it into darkness, and instigate a new Northern axis and myth. Otherwise, within a year or less, the North would cease to exist, the chemical plants would exhaust themselves and lapse, their subjugated workforce wrung to death, the cities would all fall, and only a depopulated wasteland would occupy the terrain of the North.

At that meeting, the rebels attempted to evoke the infinite myths of previous uprisings of the North, from the Dark Ages to the Jarrow March and the Thatcher-crushed Miners' Strike, along with the moments in England's history when all power had been held in the North, so that those events could be recorded in some way, to serve as an inspiration for the current uprising. But with the erasure of all history and knowledge, in its transferral from annulled paper-based media to digital data and that data's obliteration during England's economic, infrastructural and technological collapses, nothing remained, and all memory had gone. All of the tongues that could have seized the memory of past Northern uprisings had been cut out, and stamped into dirt. But that zero-memory of the past served only to propel the rebels ever more violently into the immediate future, with such velocity – there, in that darkened cinema – that the dominant rebel brigade instantly bisected itself, then proliferated into multiple new brigades, each vying urgently to precipitate England's darkness.

Only one rebel, standing in front of the cinema screen, and hallucinating with the toxic chemicals he had inhaled while traversing the urban peripheries on his way to that revolutionary assembly, managed to voice the uprising's mythical, determining origin, desperately piecing together shredded fragments of memory, an instant before they deliquesced into oblivion. He evoked – deliriously, in bursts, as though speaking in glossolalia –

a meeting that had taken place, in October 1988, at the Broadmoor hospital for the criminally insane, between the two now-dead but still-legendary 'Kings of Leeds', Peter Sutcliffe and Jimmy Savile, during Savile's era as that hospital's de-facto director, having seized power from his ostensible advisory role, at a seminal moment when, due to malfunctions of its administrative regime, the insane had ruled that asylum, sweeping-aside its directors. The two Kings of Leeds had met for profound discussions of the future, in a palatial, thickly-curtained annex of the asylum, first embracing one another warmly, then stood together, Sutcliffe's head turned attentively to Savile, two eager interpreters beside them, as though only irreconcilable idioms of madness could be voiced. But they remained silent, as though in anticipation of being photographed, like two dictators, though no image was to be made of that meeting, and its memory subsisted solely in the pixellated hallucinations of a soon-to-be-culled rebel boy, standing in front of the pornography cinema's screen, in the semen-preserved grandeur of the Assembly Rooms, his delirium now drained, but his throat still convulsing with the effort to expectorate, at last, a myth, an origin.

Finally, via that throat, Savile calmly spoke just one phrase: 'The North Will Rise Again.' Exhausted, his throat's membrane seared, the rebel fell to the ground.

From that moment, the South was doomed. An immense roar of approval split-through the cinema's walls and permeated the entire city, terrifying the young conscripts stationed in the disused turkish baths beneath the Queen's Hotel. The rebels were now certain that – with its origin in an amalgam of psychotic serial-killing and self-obsessional spectacle – their uprising could not fail.

3

The splintering of the rebel brigades into violent and inassimilably opposed factions, during their legendary conclave in the Assembly Rooms, delayed a formal declaration of civil war against the South: a moment of acute turmoil followed, in which, once again, rebel-brigades massacred one another in nihilistic abandon at the same time as they fought the governmental conscript forces with tenacity. Finally, the last-ditch survivors of a near-eliminated rebel brigade adroitly ambushed a motorcade of chemical-plant overseers and occupation-bureaucrats as they roared up the last stretch of the empty M1 motorway, complacent in their power as they anticipated the multiple sex-acts they would compel the children of the North to visit upon them. Following that ambush, the last-ditch rebels created such a spectacular display of the serially-killed and decapitated occupation-bureaucrats and overseers – stringing the bodies directly below the motorway-junction gantries announcing 'The North', and positioning the heads so they appeared to surmount the great cooling-towers of the power-stations that ran alongside that motorway – that they successfully precipitated a new massing of the Northern brigades, inspired by their uprising's originating myth, driven by all-engulfing obsession and oblivious to all rules of combat, as they now turned in fury towards the South. Until that instant, the threat of their own elimination had never occurred to the governmental, administrative, military and corporate elites, and they responded by instigating still-greater conscription of the young population of the South, so dazed by consumerism's fall that they had either been rendered bewildered and eager to die, or else ready to embrace the terminal-warfare ethos which that conflict now demanded.

A hard conflict came down on England, with no surrender conceivable on either side. Two winters of mutual attrition followed, with widescale punitive massacres conducted in areas whose populations were seen as affiliated to the rebel brigades; those populations were packed screaming into abandoned mega-malls and technology showrooms, the doors bolted and all means of escape sealed, then the buildings were incinerated by governmental death-squads, the inhabitants carbonised. The conscript forces lost over half of their number each winter, in ambushes as they moved in tactical zigzags across the Northern zonal wastelands, between the chemical-plant cities whose aluminium chimneys had been sabotaged, set on fire or put out of use. The governmental forces welcomed that reduction of the extraneous elements of their own conscript phalanxes, many of whom had grown already dispirited by the collapse of their mission, thereby rendering themselves vulnerable to immediate massacre by the rebel brigades. Only the most hardened conscripts would survive that process of reduction, and their reward would be the assignation to them, by the governmental elites, of the prized opportunity to accelerate the wastelanding and voiding of the North.

Each winter, the Northern famines grew more bitter, until they stretched all year-round; the populations, rebel brigades and conscript forces all endured the same virulent hallucinations. The eating of all remaining animals took place during the conflict's fourth winter. In that time of famine, emaciated children of four years of age would be charged by their families with the dangerous task of walking great distances, barefoot, to collect loaves of inedible sawdust bread, almost the size of the children's bodies, from the now-dispersed bakeries, then carry them home across the Northern wastelands, in terror at the prospect of being out-run by assailants, and dispossessed; a habitual sight, for travellers across those scorched-earth zones, was that of a felled, throat-slit child, lacerated feet surrounded by arcs of spat-out-again bread.

Soon, all inhabitants of those razed zones between cities fled them, and moved into the cities, if they could survive their transit through the burnt-out ruins of the toxic chemical-plants on the urban peripheries. Mass prostitution rapidly became the dominant industry of those cities, along with the provision of weaponry for the autonomous gang-warfare which still thrived among the sub-teen populations, directly alongside the incessant street-combat between the rebel brigades and the governmental conscripts, as though performed in oblique derision for those rebels' aspirations and dreams. But after the hard winters of fighting, those cities, too, were now giving-up, too disintegrated to be tenable as cities any longer, even by the laxest urban criteria, as though those once-thriving cities had reverted as entities, backwards in time, in a veering blur of speed, back beyond the conception of the world's first cities.

The Manchester rebel brigade's gnarled and alcohol-addled leader – a legendary punk-rock veteran – had just comprehensively wiped-out the Liverpool brigade in factional in-fighting, and powered by elation, led his brigade directly into a governmental conscripts' ambush, on Saddleworth Moor, his great plan to cull the Bradford brigade – after moving across the Pennines under cover of darkness – covertly betrayed to the overall commander of the governmental forces. Exhausted by the celebrations that had followed its triumph over the Liverpool brigade, and outnumbered by the well-armed conscripts, that brigade was soon obliterated, its leader decapitated, but his head, its tongue sticking-out between its toothless jaws, eyes still open and glaring, was taken up to the high moor by survivors and carefully preserved through immersal in a solution of vodka and formaldehyde, so that it resembled a feral child's, then dispatched to the Bradford brigade in an old tin box, for display in future confrontations, to strike terror into the conscript phalanxes. The civil war in the North had reached its seminal moment, as the rebel brigades waged a mercilessly brutal combat to take the coastal axis-points of Yorkshire, and liberate the remaining chemical-industry cities, with their heavily fortified grand hotels, before launching their all-out assault on the South.

The overall commander of the governmental forces in the North put on a thick overcoat and black-fur hat, left his palatial suite on the top storey of the Queen's Hotel, to give a desperate and ferociously amplified speech – from the balcony directly above the name of the hotel, incised into its vast Purbeck marble facade, which dwarfed his figure – to the contemptuous population, which had been forcibly assembled in the city square beneath that balcony, kept at a distance behind barriers by complicit kapos from the civilian population. The commander knew he had to deliver a speech able to bring that entire population over, in extremis, to the governmental forces' side, and had spent all of the previous night preparing it. His microphone wailed, battering the buildings on the far side of the square in feedback. His audience, initially restive, had grown silent. He approached the microphone and began to speak, one hand executing a slicing-fist gesture of emphasis: 'Citizens of the North! Let me speak from the heart. We have a divine mission which requires your participation... We will surpass the First World War! We will surpass even the Thirty Years War! – In genocide! In genocide! – You, the population of Leeds, we will send you out into the countryside around this city, into the blackened devil's ground, we will send you for re-education, for massacre, for culling, for "smashing"... Your next summer holiday-camp destination will be the Yorkshire Omarska.' His microphone emitted torrents of feedback, erasing his words.

The crowd hesitated for a moment, seized by the commander's vision, then his eyes abruptly reeled as he watched them storm the barriers, massacring the kapos, and attempt to infiltrate the hotel's ornate foyer and chandeliered ballroom, that initial rush repulsed only by sustained bursts of rocket fire. The commander abandoned his forces, barricaded into the turkish baths in the hotel's subterranea; he took the elevator to the roof, cursing the North from his helicopter as it pivoted over the river Aire to head southwards at speed.

4

Following the abandonment of the Queen's Hotel by the governmental forces' overall commander, and the parallel defection from the roof of the Grand Hotel in Scarborough by the oceanic-zone commander – whose helicopter malfunctioned on take-off and crashed without trace into the cold Northern seas – the concerted assault on the South began. Still without a leader, the punk-inspired rebel brigade factions aberrantly coalesced, and planned to march down the deserted M1 motorway, to raze London to the last ash. At that moment, the governmental forces, anticipating that plan and already panic-stricken at the prospect of their imminent torturing and decapitation at the brutal hands of the Northern hordes, sent light-aircraft to saturate the entire tarmac expanse of the M1 with toxic chemicals produced in the North's own factories, then ignited it, so that a voracious river of fire traversed the spine of England, emitting immense vertical flames that were visible to any omniscient spectator positioned far above the planet; those motorway flames would continue to burn – the chemicals produced had been experimental ones, designed for extreme, long-term efficacy in the future wastelanding and scorched-earthing of the North, after (or even before) it had been depopulated – until England itself had been extinguished.

Faced with that conflagration, the rebel brigades had to split into new factions and improvise their way South, in perverse tangents, dead-ends and spirals that eluded the governmental conscript forces sent to bar their way. When they did meet conscript phalanxes, the rebels massacred them mercilessly. They camped in derelict, centuries-old sanatoria, hospitals for the criminally insane, and workhouses. Once they had crossed the fellatio-determined border with the South, the population fled from them, fearing slaughter and evacuating their towns or cities to head westwards into exile, or eastwards towards ports from which they hoped to escape to mainland Europe. Within a month, the rebels' encroachment of the South had brought them close to London, and at the onset of winter, the Northern factions reconnoitred on the western side of the Thames, at Richmond Bridge. While they watched, governmental engineers approached from the far side of the river, mined the bridge and detonated it.

Massed and armed, and ready to raze London, the rebel brigades froze into stasis. They knew they now had the momentum to erase England and cast it into darkness – as a punitive reprisal for the attempted wastelanding and depopulation of the North, if any justification were necessary – by seizing and assassinating all of the governmental, administrative, military and corporate elites of the South, by obliterating those elites' strongholds around the final resonant sites of England, and by incinerating all of England's myths and casting them into irrecoverable oblivion; but at the same time, the rebel brigades wanted to prolong that sensation of the imminent engulfing of their adversary, and to ecstatically defer England's fall, as though in capricious contempt. And, during that interval of stasis, the winter abruptly came down: England's last winter, and the bitterest one of all.

The decision was taken to suspend London's razing until the following summer. Maintaining sufficient amassed power at the Thames to deter any counter-attack, the rebel brigades undertook a subterfuge bluff by appearing to retreat, allowing many of their factions to return to the North for necessary in-fighting and the violent exacerbation of territorial disputes. Rebel poets were dispatched to the most exposed and isolated terrains of the high moors, in order to formulate profound reflections – a philosophy of England's ending – while gazing down upon the wiped-out, still-fiery cities of the North, from whose decommissioned chemical-industry chimneys gushes of fire still residually emerged and pulsed high into the pristine, ultramarine skies, now so maximally contaminated that they had become pure again. The vast task of removing all consumerist debris from the building-facades and gutters of the North's surviving cities was set in motion, and a scattering of rebels was dispatched to oversee and taunt the many thousands of conscript prisoners of war assigned to the task; those prisoners worked relentlessly, by night under acetylene floodlights, until the work killed them. Other rebel factions were sent to the North's coastal zones, where renegade conscripts had assimilated themselves into the civilian populations, either for acts of guerrilla combat or to preserve their own accursed lives, and now needed to be comprehensively uprooted and culled. The rebel brigades agreed to meet again, on the banks of the Thames at Richmond, on the first day of the following summer, for the arbitrary voiding and razing of London, and the negation of England's mythic sites.

The governmental elites watched the dispersal of the rebel brigades with astonishment, uncertain whether those brigades simply disdained to take the trouble to eliminate the South, or if, by some caprice, they had granted the South a reprieve, in which to rectify its corruption, before deciding on its fate, at some unknown moment in the future. The terror of the South transformed itself into elation, and the governmental forces declared victory over the rebel brigades, announcing their expulsion back to their godforsaken Northern wastelands; several of the moribund digital image-screens surmounting London's most magnificent corporate towers were miraculously set back into operation, and films of triumph momentarily displayed, to the sceptical eyes of the still-petrified populations, who were well-aware that their reprieve could be short. Those films, on the malfunctioning image-screens, flickered diabolically, as though they were the very first film images ever projected, then the screens blew-out or turned to darkness. The populations of London knew that the rebels could return, to decimate them (any survivors of that assault would be subject to extinction or exile, exactly as the governmental forces had planned for any survivors of their own, now-overturned assault on the North). During the lull before the rebels' return, the military elites deliberated on the feasibility of sending rescue-squads to the North to extract and liberate the now-stranded and surrounded conscript phalanxes, entrenched within isolated forests or in the barricaded subterraneas of grand hotels; several rescue-squads were tentatively dispatched beyond the peripheries of London, but after their immediate capture and culling by the attentive rebel forces, all discussion of the stranded conscripts lapsed.

The winter ran its course, with iced winds wailing across the South from every side, scouring-away the skin of London's populations; all supplies of food and other resources had been blockaded by the rebel forces, so that a hard famine came down upon that city, rivalling those of the North. Then, the winter suddenly vanished, the sun appeared over the Thames from between blackened clouds, and all intimations indicated that England's coming summer would be a supremely beautiful one: the most beautiful one of all time, and the final summer, for England.

Mercy's Eyes

1

a rebel boy was ambushed in the high moor
the conscripts took him to their base in the city
– an old turkish baths in the basement of the now-derelict Queen's
Hotel –
and told him he would have seventy minutes to live

on the way into the city
he saw the chemical factories on fire in the suburbs
– turquoise and primrose flames ascending,
white heat –
and wept with joy
at the aura of devastation
at the sweetness of obliteration
of the Northern burning cities

believing the fall of that city to the rebels to be imminent
the rebel boy tried to gain time
by offering to tell the conscripts stories
in the blackest minutes of the night

every story was a story of death
– genocide, incest, mutilation, incineration,
and the story of his own massacred children –
so the conscript boys listened, enraptured

while caressing one another's penises
until the smell of semen filled the air,
leaked up through the hotel corridors
and attracted girls and animals in the burnt-out streets outside

when the time was up,
the rebel boy pleaded for mercy
and the conscripts slit his throat and stomach
cut off his testicles and threw them in the air
cut out his storytelling tongue finally,
and threw the body into the polluted river Aire:
mercy is the hardest story

2

mercy's eyes have a stare that corrodes –
the danger upon us from heaven every night

the smell of the steam from overheated bodies every day

a burning and a dissemination from some flesh

in their isolation, the conscript-occupants of the once-lavish
Queen's Hotel
(the grandiose, Ceausescu-dimensioned palace of the North),
spit and think of the voids between flesh

and they say
– it's endless, it's endless
that uniqueness

the fingers that invoked
– in their movements, to and fro –
the suppression of all mercy

the conscript boys watch the sky above the city
every night
and they try to imagine
how the attack will begin

from suppression to liberation:
the children of liberation

the rush of the combatants' exhilaration
is a weapon against –
just a weapon against,
and so they weep
just a tear against their faces

the boys look at one another
when the sky comes down
and it makes a language
which is exiled to them

long ago, tongues would break,
fabricating, making such a story

whenever the conscript boys try
to remember their sisters' loving faces
– before the hostilities –
then mercy appears, in a swarm of tenderness
that blocks out the images
of the face, before its birth

– I remember, says the boy without memory,
– a fall of golden hair, around an infant face

gesture around sex, the body, the image

to keep moving out of compulsion

the boys, shoulder to shoulder
huddled together, eye to eye –
enumerating their friends who died young
out of calculation

so – the parks, the glorious buildings
on the point of destruction
and the warmth of it all
that sends those watching eyes sunblinded

if mercy had an eye to weep with, an eye to stare with
that vision would hold
the mirage of disintegration

the boys know, if silence were unnecessary,
then they could sing
– work it up, work it up, until it shoots!
until their voices were gone forever

they are waiting to be exiled to a land
where exile is valuable

their lives have been put out
in a fire that went out, before their birth

the lives of the conscript boys
are abandoned images and crippled dance

the sky explodes in phosphorescent red –
a sun that desires and bursts in those boys' eyes

streets packed with debris of discarded consumer goods
not wide enough now
to fit in all the prostitutes
but the streets still seem immense,
the avenues marbled and physical

swans over the river –
the boys with torn eyes just dream about that
in the darkness

– our leaders have abandoned us...,
the boys cry out
it's these disintegrating skies
over the disintegrating cities
that make them feel that way

but it's true – every conscript is now in charge of his own boots
stranded without hope of rescue
every one of them, or most of them,
those hunger-crazed boys with blazing flesh

at night, under rebel bombardment
and the threat of lethal-chemical attacks
images of imagined cities
flash gratuitously, compulsively

through the boys' sensorium:
Sarajevo, Tokyo, Nanking, Dresden…

of the charred, skeletal cities of the North
this is still the strongest –
the one that resists, against the rebel forces

the boys have been dancing, in the anticipation of death:
the gush of fluids –
not again, not again,
that's a dream it takes a lifetime of dreaming
to crumble underfoot

get warmed up –
the boys rub the rotten fabric
of their governmental uniforms,
over the shy organs
until the stink of months' disuse and disease
the stench of desolation
comes to comfort them

one boy murmurs to another
at four of that horrified night
– yes, yes, we can still fuck one day
another boy responds:
– in our moment of extremity
then silence of night, again

survival is foreclosed, infinitely gone –

so the conscript boys are joyful
at every consumed moment

just before dawn:
the retch of noise, a rainbow of slivers,
then the detonation in the sleeping boys' ears

the boys reassure themselves
– we'll cut our own throats, rather than surrender
then we'll run down the street
as whirlwinds of blood, holding hands

to know mercy
to hold it with courage
when all the dreams are gone –
that is the conscript boys' desire
to penetrate mercy

the surrounding cities
– every digital image-screen now shattered –
are polluted by chemical attacks
to the point of urban brutality
you can eat the sulphur
you can drink the acid, for nourishment

the grandiose Purbeck-marbled facade
– carapaced with blast-dust,
indented with haywire missile-fire –
and shattered windows of the Queen's Hotel

form the last-ditch palace of those dispossessed boys

in their last moments, the boys believe
the streets outside have stood too long
and all the reasons for civil warfare and conflict
are just screens
for natural disintegration

in the North, there stands a city:
in the city, there stands a ruined hotel:
in the hotel basement, there stand the heated baths
that have cracked and drained away:
some fearful conscripts have taken refuge there
from the nightly conflagration
in the city above
and the heat is driving them crazy
and the punk-inspired rebel force will arrive some dawn
when the purpled incendiary sky
has cleared and gone...

terrors build new bodies
and new buildings
around those boys' bodies

the conscript boys send one of their number
up to the roof of that palatial hotel
to survey the surrounding urban terrain
and assess the rebels' advance

but the boy is instantly torn-apart by shell-fire
before his darkness-habituated eyes can focus –
and the near-collapsed roof
is ready to crack wide open
all the way to our most feared hells and half-hells,
from the physical exudation of fear
bursting out from the conscripts' bodies beneath it

sick at heart, from the malediction of their lives
the boys put their hands together
and consider one another's eyes,
searching for a means to escape

at the moment before their waking,
the boys fantasise situations
in which they are brought all they need –
then they awaken with lamentations, with nothing

the last winter was a hard one, the conflict running on,
silver and turquoise freezing skies, and solitude:
now the winter is coming again

the conscript boys tell one another
– it's foregone, that death will come to us
while we're still young
it will strike us, cut us down

in moments of hunger-hallucinated luxury
some boys dream of the touch

of a sister's blood-warm flesh
and other boys dream
that they float in the river, eyes up,
and alive, in the sun

it's said
the rebels are now at the city's edge
and an instant later,
they're already crossing the bridge over the river Aire
that had marked inviolable conscript territory,
filming that mundane traversal with an old cine-camera

now the conscript boys commit themselves
to never laying down to sleep again –
they commit their bodies
into the hands and the heart of exhaustion

and the avenues of the city
hiss with the heat of weapons,
of the attack upon them –
under rocket fire,
the hotel's facades are indented still deeper
to make a language of a thousand pitted eyes:
eyes of mercy
for the expended conscript boys

in the terror of attack,
the boys hold one another
eyes streaming hot tears

and they bite each other's lips –

for one moment,

the attack falters

(in the next moment,

the entire city will be obliterated)

and in their release

the boys lick one another's blood away

3

The rebel boys captured in the battle for the river Frome had been marched into a pear-tree grove at midday and shot, each with a bullet in the back of the neck. The heat haze was sweet with blood and flowers and pear juice.

The adolescent girls of the village by the river came to look at the bodies. They had it in for those rebel boys because they refused to fuck (too scared, or too preoccupied with their mission, it was impossible for anyone to say). The girls pulled at one another's golden braids as they spat into the rebel boys' eyes. A pear-tree was burning in the distance, gasolined branches flaring.

In the village's hotel, the regional commander of the governmental forces was fucking the prostitute which his squadron had brought along on their expedition. Outside the hotel, his conscripts were sitting in the street of dirt, eating black sausage. They had advanced from the south. The afternoon hours went by. Then the execution squad sauntered back from the pear-tree grove, blood up to their elbows. The conscripts on the ground pretended to taunt them: 'You inhuman pigs!' As everyone laughed, the commander was shooting his semen into the anus of the squadron's prostitute. He gave a cry of death and wept hot tears that spattered onto the girl's skin and ran down her spine. Then he cried out: 'I have forces that are over two hundred strong!

I'm a man to be reckoned with!' The girl looked at the wall. It hurt, it hurt...

In due course, the commander gathered up his conscripts and they moved out of the village in a convoy. They crossed the bridge over the foaming, polluted river, where the village girls were bathing naked, holding the rebel boys' bodies in their arms. Those boys had refused to fuck the golden-haired village girls – and so had been betrayed by the girls to the governmental forces – because they insisted on being faithful to the red-haired girls in their home cities, close by the cold black Northern sea. It was all they could do to stop their hearts bursting out of their bodies with love for those fierce girls. Each boy had joined the punk-inspired rebel forces at the age of thirteen or fourteen. As they left their cities, the rebel boys pleaded with their girls to stay true. They said: 'Even if we go through hell, if we pass through every massacre, we will return.'

By the time the rebel boys had passed the perimeters of their cold cities, their girls had the semen of the trawler-crew boys running out of their mouths and anuses, and down their thighs. But they were true. They told themselves: 'We'll pass through every trawler-crew on the Northern coast until we've exhausted them all. Then our rebel boys will return to us.' They wiped the trawler-crew boys' semen from their lips, but relenting, deposited it on their tongues and swallowed it down.

The golden-haired village girls beside the river Frome knew nothing of this story. They just believed that the rebel boys had been too terrified to fuck, knowing the governmental forces' desire to massacre them. As they bathed in the river with the rebel boys' bodies, the girls kissed the entry wounds in the boys' necks and stroked their penises, to comfort them on the journey into hell. Finally, they released the bodies to flow into the acid-laced current.

Stepping out of the river into the evening sunlight, the girls threw their arms around one another, wailing: 'Nobody will fuck us! Nobody!' All of the village boys of their age had already died cruel deaths while serving as conscripts in the governmental forces, massacred by other factions of governmental forces in the course of tactical exercises.

But the girls remembered with joy that the local asylum housed a dozen cretin boys who were exempt from conscription into the governmental forces. They ran naked through sunflower fields to the asylum, to fuck the cretin boys.

Naturally, the cretin boys wanted to be paid for their time. But the village girls tricked them, distributing a tin coin marked 'no value' to each cretin boy as his semen streamed down each girl's windpipe, or into their anuses. By the time the cretin boys discovered the deception, their testicles had been squeezed void. The golden-haired village girls carried home the cretin boys' semen in their throats and anuses, or desiccating in the space between their breasts.

For the cretin boys, this was just one more disappointment among a thousand others. How they hated the hell of an exploited life. All they wanted was money to hire nurses to read stories to them. The next morning, a 'sanitation force' co-sponsored by two rival phalanxes of the governmental forces took the cretin boys away to a derelict warehouse and massacred them, each with a bullet in the back of the neck. The grinning bodies were left to rot, except for the penises, which were fairly distributed among the sanitation force, as trophies.

Out on the black Northern sea, the trawler-crew boys gazed out along the coast, where immense fireballs shot upwards from the incinerated cities. Even from out at sea, screams could be heard. The lights of the trawler-crew's home port shone brightly. The night and the sea were freezing. The trawler-crew boys considered the situation, and decided to stay out at sea a little longer.

4

two adolescent conscripts
trapped a rebel in the wasteland between two abandoned cities
doused his head in precious gasoline
which they ignited
while sodomising him

on the horizon,
the world exploded again
in a roaring gasoline hell
– the imminent extinguishment of all petrol, all oil,
made it all the more enticing to squander,
in great quantities, in vast spectacles –

it's so banal, for the conscript boys,
that relentlessly ongoing apocalypse

the conscript boys chant
while rubbing the spilt semen and blood
into their fatigues
– the atrocity of it all,
and the beauty of it all...

above all, they prized
the beauty of the soft skin

between the rebel boy's testicles

and the beauty of his head of ashes

of his laid-bare teeth

of his still-burning eyelashes

ascending into the void

above this land:

England

5

the mothers of the rebel boys have been carbonised
the girls of the rebel boys have been carbonised
their bastard children have been carbonised, too

those boys have a genealogy of ashes
this land has a genealogy of ashes
this world has a genealogy of ashes

the trawler-boys finally came ashore from the sea
– when their itching made their black world blaze –
and the governmental forces immediately ordered them
to capture an ochre river, a tributary of the Humber
– so dense with sediment, oil-residue and debris
it seemed to those boys to be an infernal river of near-solidified
blood and excrement –
and of no strategic importance whatsoever

a brigade of rebel boys immediately mobilised,
perceiving the trawler-boys to be collaborators,
and massacred those boys from the Northern sea
while they were preoccupied with their aching testicles,
so now, the boys from the sea are floating down the ochre blood
river,
towards their beloved open sea

it's said, also,
that all of the girls of the conscript boys
have been massacred
(almost without exception)
in their absence
and the conscript boys have been holding their throats,
murmuring:

– our hearts will break apart now
for lack of mercy, now our girls are dead
and must be resuscitated, from ashes,
from all they have passed through,
from soot, bones, carbon,
from the vanishing of flesh:
by our love, by our love...

a genocide-intent commander of the conscript boys
was betrayed by a cabal of his own forces
while drinking Coca-Cola in the restaurant of a luxury hotel,
and after he was machine-gunned in the back
his head was taken off with a machete blow
and then paraded in that city's streets
to the delight of the rebels' sympathisers,
then the remainder of the carcass was incinerated
at a municipal institution in the suburbs,
the ashes were then trampled underfoot
into the most minute carbonised bone splinters
and dispersed by the rebel sympathisers
to the bleakest, most barren fields of England,
and given to the wind
to carry away,
while the frightened bystanders averted their eyes

a bad winter came down on the North
hunger, ashes and ice everywhere
and a big orange sun came up in the sky
for twenty hours in every godforsaken day,

then the ochre blood river turned into a frozen network
of arterial spasms
– the disintegrated nervous system of that land –
until it cracked wide open, in springtime,
gushing red fluids, body parts,
shotguns, teeth, fingernails:
a river of life

at night in the conscripts' stronghold city,
the most menial conscript
fucks the most luxurious prostitute
while squeezing her nipples
and after he fills her anus with his semen,
she sucks at his penis
until he shoots semen into her eyes
while she screams out:
– I love you, I love you...

7

everyone knows that girl is wild
the last survivor of the conscripts' girls
(the exception)
and she will take revenge upon us
– we, the surviving rebel boys –
for our inept manoeuvres,
for our failed attempts,
to carbonise her, in the end

Liberation's Ashes

1

My sister Beatrice was scalpelled to death at the age of fourteen in a gangwarfare skirmish, during the eradication of England. I have survived and grown to maturity, in my exile, only to recount our story. We were born into that strange city of precarious and blistered tenements in the North-East of England; one side was the sea, on the other side was the moors, coloured, according to the movement of the light, primrose, blood-red, black, white, and slate-grey. The violence of that miserable void city was so intense, you could feel it snapping at your feet from the very earth itself. The noise of the malfunctioning urban-transit system cracked, shuddered and screamed along the two-bit streets and avenues, and the city was already agonising from dawn until two the next morning, just from the cacophony of it all. The greatest blessing of my life is that I no longer live in that city, but I am still its cracked and exiled voice, its bad and broken spore.

I have a black universe of hatred inside me – if I can get it out of my abdomen through remembering and spitting out those gangwarfare adventures, so much the better for the people I meet in these streets of mainland Europe. The only way the children could survive in that city was by grouping together – amalgams of blows and lust – to invent new weapons with which to decapitate other groups who were sharing that cursed tenement life. It was a life so atrociously bitter, even when we weren't fighting – then we were searching for aluminium bits, for plastic fragments that could be exchanged for scraps of money (luxuriously designed old banknotes, featuring images of the heroes of England, that were now worth nothing at all).

My memory is that we were all beaten down to nothing, to pulp and shards, in our teenage years. We had the worst gang in that city, Beatrice and I, but she was strong, courageous. She would say: 'Let's erase some of the bruised history of this fucked world.' The exhausted city, as with the entire expanse of the North, had already been in murderous turmoil for years, traversed end to end by massacring brigades. As I held Beatrice in my arms each night in the shadow of the tenements, she would whisper her plans: 'We'll gather up the bones of England's dictators and lose them in an unmarked site – somewhere in the pear-tree groves, where the earth is too hard, ever to dig up again. Then we can have some fun. Otherwise, we'll be here forever in this city that must have been designed for the obliteration of our joy. Our obsessions will murder us, each dawn, in this hard country. It's all burning up. But we could live anywhere, you and I, in liberation, in some perfect city.' Beatrice was looking out at that city, dreaming about her life.

In my exile in mainland Europe, I saw its collapsed cultures resuscitated. But in England, the arena of collapse engulfed my eyes indelibly, and that is now my entire vision. Beatrice would say from the depth of her hallucinated sleep: 'How can we find a city that is not disintegrated? And if we do not, how will we survive?' I still do not know the answer to that girl's questions. They have obsessed me all my life, as I have moved from one petrified European city to another. Only the black dirt outside the cities remains strong and tested.

At night in that city, on an old wire bed without blankets or mattress, Beatrice would wind her stockinged feet around the back of my neck, and I would bite and suck at her slit while she called wildly into herself: those were the most disappointed, dispirited nights. At dawn, we would peer into the wrecked lobbies of the city's once-palatial hotels, where, for a hundred years or more, businessmen had drunk black coffee and alcohol while discussing acts of corruption. I knew all the city's orphan boys by their scars and their names – they ignored me, but Beatrice they revered as 'the girl who wants to kill us all'. Entire districts of that city had been demolished by governmental forces for no reason and replaced by fortified buildings already irreversibly cracked and falling; other parts of the city were indented and damaged by battles between the punk-inspired rebel forces' factions. The child prostitutes nourished themselves on the desiccated semen which ran in lines along their thighs, and on the guts of exhausted animals. All of those children yearned for a time in the past when it was still possible to buy drugs named 'ecstasy' and 'crack' with the gains of prostitution; but they doubted the memories of those who recounted such luxuries. They could only conclude, that cities had always been void.

A storm arrived from the moors or the sea each afternoon, to pound the dregs of our lives into oblivion. Any able-bodied adults who remained in that city, having declined to join one of the rebel factions at the conflict's origin (Beatrice and I were too young to do so), now lay down on their backs, in the grit and dirt of the avenues, and let the stormwater drown them. As they died, the curious would kneel and listen to their last words. At their moment of death, the injustice of their lives' extinguishment would appear to them as a revelation, and they would murmur: 'It's only by the most minute accident that this is not the richest, most luxurious city in the world.' Then they opened their mouths to swallow enough polluted water to die. The curious opened their mouths too, in astonished incomprehension. Beatrice closed her eyes to those spectacles, since her dreams would be tainted by lies or by flesh.

3

We took a journey by a near-empty train at night, I don't remember where. The remaining lights of the city were flashing all around us: on the rivers, on the buildings, with carbon and acid in the air. Beatrice complained hour by hour of the black and sore membranes of her body. I touched the hot ashes hanging in the air as we passed through the sites of the governmental forces' massacres and elimination camps. Beatrice said: 'Only the ashes will remember this time, this moment of passage. The cinders will find their own passage through this godforsaken world.' In the wastelands between cities, the two points at each extreme of the journey's trajectory were unknown. That journey was cooked down to the black and broken ashes of our existence, as we moved through the derelict stations at an hour when the night was packed dense and raw with the gestures of torture in those imminently depopulated cities. The train accelerated with the noise of a blood gush; we were immersed in that cacophony. At each station we stopped at, the shreds of redundant banknotes were mixed-in with the fragments of bones, the platforms covered with a debris of all of the incinerated remains of that land's history.

Beatrice said: 'Too many existences have been packed together, and their grinding has made the conflagration soar upwards, here. The ashes of all human bodies have now been placed in a hole, or thrown into the ochre blood river.' She had salt in her lips, and rust too – but that was nothing compared with the lacerations on the faces of the other, isolated passengers. It looked like their mouths had been sucking razored coins that had scraped off too many skin cells. Their intended destination was the city of Leeds, but the railway no longer reached that city, and that was a mercy for them. At dawn, the journey was over, the locomotive revolved on a turntable at an unknown city's edge, and we remained on the train for its return back to our city, the following night, to renew our participation in gangwarfare activities.

4

In those gangwarfare battles, Beatrice was always the one to strike first, and most fearlessly: her fingernails were ripped into splinters from the fury of her exhilarated blows. If she had been old enough to join one of the rebel brigades and fight the governmental forces, she would have obliterated them all, in no time. In our city, the shadow of every tenement was something to be fought for. By the age of ten, at the start of England's conflict, I had a compulsion of love for the chaos of cracked facades that were meticulously spray-canned with a weaponry of threats and names (along with drawings of devil-heads). After each battle, Beatrice would inscribe the names of her victims and her preferred phrase: 'I have seen your return from hell.' Most of the children of our age wanted to escape the conflict and become economic exiles in Germany, the land of Hitler, and so they tested out their language skills by inscribing on those facades: 'zugleich', 'zusammen', 'jetzt fertig'.

I always wanted the moment of eradication that would finally signal our victory; then, immediately afterwards, Beatrice and I could have left that land too, as on the trans-Europe train journeys that we sometimes hallucinated. But in the end every battle was lost, and victory postponed, since we could only ever marshal together for our gang the outcasts, the cripples, and the inbred of that city. It was a lonely combat, strung out and vivisected by the lack of food. We would go down to the sea each day and wash the sparks of blood from our hands; as the sun came up, it thawed the violence out of our fingernails and furnaced our bodies, instilling dangerous new hallucinations in our vision (riding on a battered bus with the wind through the open window carrying the smell of olive and cypress groves onto our skins). I was ready to give in to such a hallucination, but Beatrice trod it underfoot: she never believed it was possible to survive on hallucinations. We would wander through the tenements, collecting our daily refuse, until the night fell and our lives began again.

In that city, all lips had become numb from over-use, and fallen silent, so I had all the time in the world for dreams and hallucinations. I had a dream of the moors each night: the great stones on the high moor meshed into an arrangement of limbs, with fire somewhere below my feet. It was that derelict and hallucinatory heat that put my obsessions together and made me wonder what could constitute survival, the fragments of everything having already been destroyed. The pull of that idea of survival led me back to imagining a panicked girl, sulking by the tenements: a girl going nowhere and into the fire of that nowhere with an extremity of narcotic exhilaration (while screaming: 'Never again!'), and suffering a sickness of all those chemicals that needed to be spat out now. All of her sisters had died from that sickness.

In Beatrice's tiny room, which I shared, she had sellotaped to one paint-peeled wall a photograph of two silk-suited dictators, seated in silence together in the darkening salon of a luxurious but tainted palace. And on the facing wall, she had sellotaped photographs of the grave-sites of England's last four heroes – Blake, Churchill, Lawrence and Jarman – each photograph inscribed in charcoal strokes with a violent 'X' of negation.

Beatrice had also found a scrap from the map of an inaccessible, unknown territory within the high moors far to the west of our city, and noted down the names of four places: Muker, Hardraw Scar, Low Row, and Stalling Busk. She said: 'I will travel to each of these places in turn, and live a quiet life there. All I need is one more gangwarfare battle to give me the momentum for the journey. That will be such ecstasy, so banal.'

All through the night, I was face to face with the ghosts of our mother and father. And then back with Beatrice, on the hard ground. I could feel that she was preparing the battle in her dreams. As a prelude, she called a momentary truce between all of the factional gangs of our city, and organised an attack upon a well-defended group of American 'specialists' who (on the initiative of the over-optimistic governmental forces) were already assessing the post-conflict potential of our ruined land, even before it had been fully destroyed. The extermination of the specialists took place suddenly, while I watched from one side. The blood flowed down the dirt-stricken avenues towards the sea. Beatrice distributed the passports to her associates, keeping one for herself and one for me ('place of birth: Altadena, California'). The factional gangs then immediately separated again into mutual acrimony and hostility, driven by the heat of their oncoming massacres.

5

Now that the disintegration of England is long-accomplished, I must wait to die in a city to which I do not belong. I have spent my life as an exile from the calamity of Beatrice's death, constantly moving through Europe's borders, which have grown harder and more malicious as they passed into deeper flux. The lands of England are all Beatrice's teardrops now: all fallen. In my anger in exile, I will allow myself to be cleansed – racially, economically, physically – until I will only be bone in the streets of a frozen city. At that moment, in two or three days from now, I will be able to recall the existence of Beatrice with some strength. But then, I will not be able to record my memories.

Blinded for years by the loss of Beatrice, I hallucinated Europe as a mass of orange and golden trajectories along which I could travel, devoting myself obsessively to the recollection of Beatrice's violet eyes. Those glowing cities rejected me, and I could never find a city of liberation, alone. So my journeys became saturated with fury, as the territories of Europe appeared to blaze around me. Along the Allee der Kosmonauten in Berlin, I had the sensation that the outcome for Europe, too, would soon be England's movement into darkness, obliteration – accelerating into a chaos of dissection, with the incineration of one country after another. At least, then, Europe could lay in ruins again, dismantled and void, but perfect. I have been overtaken by

Europe, in my exile, and my toes and fingers have been blackened by it. All I hope is that the compulsion to visualise Beatrice will survive me.

When the night started to come down, Beatrice ripped the photograph of the two dictators from her wall, and slid it deep inside her coat. Then she took the passport of the American 'specialist' from my hands, inspected it closely, and said: 'If by chance I am slaughtered in tonight's skirmish, you must leave the North immediately. You cannot survive here alone. You must cross the sea and cut a path through Europe, until you fall exhausted from your travelling, or are harvested in some ethnic or sexual cleansing.' She would have lectured me more, but at that moment, her last orgasm struck her as I held one arm around her waist, my tongue in her slit, and she dropped the passport to the ground.

I whispered into Beatrice's ear: 'I promise you I will be lonely, I promise you I will be lonely' (though I was convinced, in my stupidity, that if one of us was to be slaughtered, it would be me). Later, I discovered that a trace of semen had obliterated the name of the defunct specialist. I wrote in my own name, in scarlet crayola.

Beatrice tried to marshal her inbred gang without success; they knew there could be no satisfactory conclusion to their lives – even if they died heroically, and went off to hell, things would still be tough in the North. Beatrice's plan had been to ambush another gang in a mud thoroughfare at the city's periphery. But while she was waiting to attack, hidden in the shadow of the tenements, a storm of black water and dirt shards came down from the brutal sky, discouraging Beatrice's gang and pounding their void heads. They started to shout, in despair: 'We want Coca-Cola! We want genocide! We want Fanta!' Their disheartening was total. Beatrice cried out: 'You can only fight in anger and silence!' That gang was turning its razors on its own throats.

The strongest gang in the city came down the peripheral dirt-thoroughfare, carrying old tin cans and the labels from dried-blood sausage. Its leader approached Beatrice and told her: 'If this city had been a rich and fashionable one, it would have been reparable to massacre a few specialists. But you drove us to the wrong act. You are a terrorist, worse than the governmental forces – you are dangerous.' I pressed against the wall of the tenement in abjection. I could feel the structure trembling towards its collapse. Beatrice was set upon ineptly, stabbed by chance in an artery while she cursed and lashed out lifelong scars to her assailants. The children scattered, and I cradled Beatrice's head for a moment in the filth of the city night. Then I ran, heading for the nearest port of exile, where I could take a decommissioned oil-tanker to mainland Europe. In the morning, a governmental punitive force – alerted by the disappearance of the specialists and intent on indiscriminate revenge – arrived and slaughtered every gangwarfare fighting child, without exception, then threw their bodies into the sea.

7

On the sea-journey from England, I dreamed a dream of Beatrice's death, as though I were a bystander:

one surviving witness to the trajectories of blood moved a set of fingernails, gesturing through the sequences of razor strokes and the movements of tongues that threw out cities, towards the acid imprinted into the dirt of the high moors – in the basement of the ruined hotel, the surviving governmental forces made intricate plans for the evacuation of the city and then abandoned them immediately, cutting the plans into fragments to be burned or eaten: the collapse of the city would have to proceed with its own momentum, broken by every instant – the flesh of the inhabitants carried the arena of imprecations, images and exhalations that made up the language of the city, always to be expelled... but every witness to the expulsion of every living cell from the city told a story that split from the skin to the bone, so that stories of flesh became stories of concrete and the skin of the story turned into a chemical carapace that, once animated, was feral – godforsaken in its wildness and its cries of disenchantment (only the pulses attached to the exteriorisation of fluids could maintain any level of life), and in its willingness to be submerged by any means invented, without premeditation – at the instant of Beatrice's death, the children held each other's hands in the streets of dirt that led directly from the edge of the sea, through the tracks of animals tethered to the doors of concrete tenements: every dialogue in those streets zigzagged through questions of survival, uprooting a spit of escape, obliteration, dreams of work in the rancorous acid factories of western Europe, thoughts of big cars, curses, hunger of the abused sensorium: it's a hell of refused options to be regurgitated and swallowed to infinity, in such a city, and every curse exclaimed is the same curse: sounds that come up from the stomach and enter the throat as ashes, then simultaneously expel themselves from the body and descend back into the body: it is the children who remember with the greatest intensity, but they are not the surviving witnesses and will not contemplate a new life (it's more amenable in their void of death, it's the luxury they cling to, along with their scars), while the witnesses who survive are blind and dumb, immersed in their upheavals, sitting in chairs in forgotten rooms or else scratching in black ditches, sick and back again – the children alone could verify their acts of witness, but nothing exists now of their fury and wretchedness (no act of massacre was more clinical and total, leaving no resistance, in any beating heart), and any foot that ever walked the avenues, any foot that ever walked the city streets, could give no veracity to that movement, that pressure and its endurance: the weaponry of the children was itemised after the operation, with attention to its capacity to inflict raw wounds and make an image of that rawness... and the most rusted items were placed in an archive of suppressed objects that never opened and immediately fell into terminal disrepair, while the governmental agents of the children's slaughter took turns to come and spit at the archive's door as a sign of their pride at work that had been accomplished (though no word could ever be put to paper on the subject, and a silence would be maintained until all memory of the children's existence had been shredded or blackened): for any witness to survive, their powers of speech and writing would have to be removed in a summary process, their fingernails removed too (though a new set would grow again, as an index of oblivion, cut to the quick and filed) and their teeth and tongues placed under surveillance, monitored for activity from time to time, and the chair or ditch would be the axis of a network of eyes that followed all visual traces of that betraying, verifying body: but the fingernails have a movement, that shows how the children were overturned, their bones pressed together in bizarre constructions, at the wrong angles, one against another, the shards placed under the rocks at the sea's edge, to deter interlopers, or more generally jettisoned into the sea, or else embedded into the vast letters of acid that spelled-out the name of England's final dictator, between the sheerest moor's summit and the derelict sheep-pens beneath it: the witness to the children's battles exuded the heat of a gesture, showing a face that had split, the marks of malnourishment, the ferocity of Beatrice and I (her brother), whose legs propelled deficient kneecaps, the sickle of blood, a panic, a flash of the sun, a recollection of meat, and a tear: that gesture repeated, from the blindness and brokenness of a last witness who still wanted to talk and seize survival, in his exile in Europe, but only had the most remote and minuscule remnants of the event to work with, then running against the wall, retina torn, fingers numbed – the governmental agents of oblivion have been engaged in a battle as wild as that of the children of that city, and for memory to survive now, it has to project itself inside each act of suppression, each of the acts of humiliation that overtook those children (acts of incitement, since if no initial provocation had existed, those children would not have hung on to every image of economic enticement and would have spent their time exploring the high moors, cutting the throats of now-unguarded sheep, without fury or compulsion): as they suffered their extinguishment, the children imagined all of the roads and railway tracks that would have taken them to their desired destination (dreams of those railway stations – Thirsk, Northallerton – marked as the puncture points on the spine of the North, indentations from blunt syringes, through which nothing could be pumped into that failed body, and dreams of hard currency with the power to buy neonised artefacts, movements of fluids, some kind of escape, once more), and all those networks gave out neural signals of movement to the dying brain, that needed above all to go on a journey, through a rough terrain: the cries of the children (Beatrice alone remained silent, at her moment of death) now dried up in ashes, until nothing remained of the larynx, only the entanglement of bone with the last images of life...

8

One winter later, so I've heard, our city fell to the punk-inspired rebel factions, and every last conscript of the governmental forces who guarded or occupied that city, was slaughtered.

Without my sister Beatrice, I lived in liberation's ashes. Travelling from one country to another in Europe, I experienced the loss of my escape together with the loss of Beatrice's fiery flesh. That girl had always complained how everything in the city between the sea and the moors was so banal, so mundane. But the leaking of exhilaration on my journeys across Europe had a far greater intensity of poignant banality. All through the winters, I kept moving out of terror. At night in every railway station, I was harassed, beaten, splitlipped by diseased knuckles; if I ever got to sleep, it was to awaken a moment later in a hallucination of anguished mortality. I had two banknotes from my home city, and hoarded them throughout those winters; finally, when I was certain that I was nearing a state of terminal starvation, I exchanged them in a wasteland beside the Keleti railway station in Budapest. In return, I received the smallest, most worthless coin in existence, which was immediately stolen from me, then thrown into the gutter in disgust by the thief. In the Bratislava underpasses, I tried to recount the story of my life in return for a little money to buy food, but my narrative never got beyond the first stuttered and stalled words: 'My sister Beatrice was scalpelled to death...'

9

After many years lost in Europe, I received a battered postcard from Beatrice, postmarked 'England's Darkness', and stamped with the date of her death:

forgive me
for leaving you
on a cheap scalpel blade
and remember me
always
in void europa
my only love
my wild angel
from the zoo of your world
to mine

Over the years, I found shadows of tenements in which to rest, out on the edges of the great cities of Europe. With no image of Beatrice to sustain me, I had to constantly imagine her cries, her gestures, the first lines of wretchedness which had already begun to indent themselves into her face; but all that faded fast, and I was left without the girl's body, only with her name and the recollection of her raw violence. I found an abandoned building to live in, and looked out through the window at the children embracing in the streets of a city that was mesmerised by its own oblivion.

I have recalled my fragments of Beatrice as that city disintegrates around me: the entirety of Europe is now disintegrating, in violence. In this city, too, the rebel brigades have obliterated the conscript armies for day after day on the city's periphery, and the fall is coming. The rebel forces' bombardments have destroyed every building around me but my own; the citizens have panicked, and are cutting their own throats. The conscripts have surrendered, hoping to be mercifully killed with a bullet in the heart or anus. A time of immense prostitution and rape is approaching. The sky is golden and turquoise, rich with the stink of massacres, blood and ashes. I am setting out on another journey across Europe, back to what was once England, back to my now-vanished Northern city, the moors and the sea. I have the name of my sister with me.

England's Darkness

1

On the first day of the summer of England's darkness, all of the North's rebel brigades returned from their journeys of the previous winter, and massed at the edge of London, on the far side of the Thames, at the former site of Richmond Bridge. The brigades who had remained at that site all through the winter, to deter any counter-attack from the governmental forces, glared at the rebels as they returned, as though those absentees had spent all of the intervening months indulging themselves, while the rebels left at the bridge had endured denudation and starvation. All of those returning rebels – even those who had spent the winter engaged in vitriolic in-fighting with rival factions, in the voided alleyways of the cities of the North – had undertaken profound, sustained reflections on England's imminent fall, and had deliberated on the optimal means to end England with all-erasing finality. After perversely deferring that foregone fall, to seize a time-annulled ecstasy from its suspension, those leaderless brigades – their initial punk-rock era veteran instigators culled long ago, either in bad-blood quarrels or in confrontations with the governmental conscript phalanxes – now had to execute it.

Above all, the rebel poets assigned to the high moors had deliberated intensively on the final stage of the North's uprising, as they gazed down from the precipices above Hardraw Scar and Stalling Busk, from which all of the cities of the North could be viewed, from the most obliterated, carbonised ruins that could no longer be named cities, to those which had retained their core infrastructure during their years of occupation by the governmental forces, their peripheries now turned to blackened wastelands as the final chemical plants cracked-open. In their desire to envision England's fall with the maximum lucidity – while resolutely blacking-out the time after that fall, in order to retain intact the nihilistic violence which that fall demanded – the rebel poets made compulsive journeys westwards and eastwards along the high moors' spine, across the Pennines and then back towards the cold black Northern seas, existing solely on sheep's-milk cheese and gradually descending into wild hallucinations of starvation as their supplies became exhausted. Finally, at the winter's end, their deliberations completed, they descended from the high moor and entered the North's all-but-demolished coastal cities.

Those poets returned to the Thames crossing-point guarding a precious document which they showed, for an instant only, to the massed rebel factions: the 'map of England's darkness'. That document would be the seminal instrument of England's fall. It had been discovered in the most obliterated of the North's coastal cities, hidden deep inside the coat of a legendary but nameless teenaged rebel fighter who had been covertly assassinated, stabbed with a stiletto, a year or so earlier, by a collaborationist gang, reputedly incited or even formed from conscript infiltrators, her body then stored indefinitely in the refrigeration unit of a fish-processing factory that overlooked the Northern seas, and transformed into a mythic icon of the rebels' resistance against their governmental adversaries. In the cavernous cold-room in which her body was stored, her eyes remained open with horror at the suddenness of her death – the gold-flecked, violet irises still vivid – and her pale lips were poised at the edge of a curse. The near-comatose surviving inhabitants of that city provided only the most eroded information on her identity and history, to the starvation-hallucinating poets who had arrived from the high moors. They made no distinction at all between the civil-war and the gang-warfare which had simultaneously convulsed that city; in the history of that city, all past events had become obliviously blurred into equivalence, apart from its liberation from the governmental forces. All they knew, was that she and her now-disappeared brother had saved that city from certain, total obliteration (it still existed, albeit only by a hair's-breadth), and when they had moved her body to the cold-room, to preserve it until such time that a mausoleum could be constructed, and opened her coat to venerate her wound, that document had been found. Whether she herself had drawn the map, or whether she had received it from a supreme tactical leader of the rebel brigades who had been slaughtered in the previous winters, and forgotten, was unknown.

The map of England's darkness was rapidly confiscated from the rebel poets and studied by all of the Northern factions. It had been drawn haphazardly in charcoal strokes, with four territorial axis-points, highlighted with jagged arrows and the inscription of four names, all located in the South. The North was rendered in dense, zigzagged strokes, as though to signal that its liberation had been completed, or else that it was now such a scorched-earth wasteland, after the previous years' conflict, that it could no longer be represented. The map had been drawn on the reverse of a monochrome photographic print showing the meeting, in October 1978, between two dictators, Nicolae Ceausescu and Pol Pot, both in silk suits, seated in identical armchairs in the lavish, high-ceilinged salon of a governmental palace, each resting their arms on the sides of their armchairs and looking down towards the carpet, fixedly and at a tangent, instead of at the camera or at one another; their eager interpreters stood behind them, ready to assist, but those twinned figures had evidently remained utterly silent until that point in their encounter. None of the rebels who gazed at the photograph could identify the two figures, but all agreed, that here were two men reflecting profoundly on genocide at punk-rock's optimum moment of derangement, and that, at the very next instant, Ceausescu would turn his head attentively towards Pol Pot, who would then calmly speak just one phrase: 'The North Will Rise Again'.

The map inscribed on the photograph's reverse face now determined the rebel brigades' plan for the uprising's last phase. They would immediately seize and obliterate all four of England's resonant, mythic axis-points – as indicated by the map – and jettison the amassed bones of its four final heroes: 'England's four rascals', as they were called in an afterthought annotation scrawled at the edge of the map, but all of them barely known to the Northern rebels, who understood only that those four figures embodied England, contrarily, in all of its grandiose aberrations and perversions. And they were now decided, that they would blindly follow, to its end, the map of England's darkness.

In addition, the Northern factions decided to appoint, as their leader, for the final assault on the South's governmental elites, the rebel among them who most closely resembled the description (a hallucinated, fractious one, at best), provided by their exhausted and starved poets, of the face and eyes of the assassinated cartographer in the coastal factory cold-room; that leader would incorporate the still-living presence, among the Northern factions, of the prescient deviser of England's fall. Until that point, all of those factions' great successes, in culling the conscript phalanxes and preparing the subjugation of the South, had been due to the violent dynamics of their instinctual, leaderless formation, but now, for the following of that map to its conclusion, they needed a resolute, guiding eye. They chose an already battle-hardened, seventeen-year-old fighter named Iris – with a distinguished punk-rock lineage, her progenitors all wiped-out in the nihilistic, factional in-fighting among the rebel brigades – who now inherited and held the map of England's darkness.

Along with the map of England's darkness, the rebel poets who descended from the North's coastal cities had also brought with them a loving captive: Gary Glitter, whose spectacular, repetition-powered cacophonies of the early 1970s had razed the sonic ground in preparation for punk-rock's psychotic outbursts and its seminal ethos of sensory oblivion. Glitter, now in his late seventies, had been performing a last-ditch show for the conscript occupiers, in a disintegrated oceanside ballroom, when the rebel poets stormed the venue and rapidly machine-gunned the entire conscript audience, leaving the bullet-riddled, open-mouthed bodies sprawled across their once-plush seats. Glitter initially feared for his life, too, but the rebel poets immediately recognised him and kissed his feet in adulation. Before the conflict, Glitter had been abominated for obsessional sex-crimes, many of them undertaken in intimate collusion with the 'King of Leeds', Jimmy Savile, but after four years of civil-war upheavals and reversals, sex-crime had become embedded so deeply into the urban landscape, and scarred pervasively into every human body, in immense genealogies of prostitution, rape and sexual murder, that it now appeared the most natural and habituated of human acts. The rebel poets invited Glitter to join them on their journey back to the rebel factions' headquarters beside the Thames. Now, clad in a skin-tight silver jumpsuit, he was appointed the 'prince of England's darkness' by the massed Northern hordes, and, as night fell, heart terminally bursting with exhilaration, he performed *Rock'n'Roll (Part 2)* at such thunderous, excessively amplified volume that birds fell stunned from the sky, eardrums shattered, and walls split apart.

As the sonic shockwaves of *Rock'n'Roll (Part 2)* slowly faded, the Northern rebels fired a high-velocity explosive rocket across the Thames, to alert the governmental forces to the initiation of their uprising's final phase. The terrified governmental elites followed the rocket's south-easterly flight, until it detonated within the already-abandoned Bentall shopping-mall in Kingston-upon-Thames, creating a vast black hole, identical in dimensions to Ubehebe Crater in Death Valley, California, and eradicating that once-glorious structure, so comprehensively that not even dust, smoke or debris remained.

2

That night, an advance-guard of the rebel forces infiltrated London, crossing the Thames by the nearest bridge to the south, at Kingston, under cover of darkness, though the rocket explosion had terrorised the area's governmental conscript guards, and they had fled from the area around the bridge. The vast crater created by the rocket's detonation was located close to the bridge, and once the rebels had crossed, they stood at the crater's lip and looked down into it, under moonlight. A fissure had been breached between the Thames and the impact-site, and river-water now poured into the crater, submerging the layered, pulverised foundations of all of the buildings which had ever occupied that site. Within minutes, the water filled that crater to its maximal extent, then overspilled it. The rebels observed that, along with the water, hundreds of human bodies – pulverised as comprehensively as the buildings' foundations – were being disgorged over the crater's lip, propelled in a tidal-wave towards the heart of London.

The rebels soon realised that, in anticipation of their incursion, the city's surface layer had already been almost entirely voided by the governmental forces. The rocket-impact had only confirmed, to the South's governmental, administrative, military and corporate elites, that the surface of their capital was already lost. Since the onset of the previous winter, they had instituted immense construction projects within London's subterranea, to re-locate the city's starving inhabitants, along with its essential infrastructure, underground; the conscript forces, merged with the city's population, would then conduct corrosive guerrilla warfare against the infiltrating Northern rebels, over years or decades if necessary, emerging at night through gaps or manholes to assassinate one or two rebels at a time, until all of those brutal invaders had been overcome, throat-slit or dispatched back to their wastelands. The governmental elites had dug vast excavation works and tunnels around the already-intricate configuration of London's lost-rivers and sewers, incorporating a miniature railway that would transport those elites from one subterranean region to another; most of the city's population, together with its conscript forces, were re-housed in shacks within those tunnels and sewers. The compacted layers of many centuries of construction under the city's corporate towers had been comprehensively assessed, with the discovery of sprawling networks of well-protected rooms, offices and command-centres, dating from previous conflicts and equipped with air-filtering systems connected to the surface-level; although those filtration networks had not been operational for many decades, the governmental elites instructed their engineers to reactivate them, and to dig ever deeper. Since the previous winter, London had become a thriving subterranea-city, its population now almost totally habituated to a life in near-darkness, protected from the feared onslaught by the brutal Northern invaders. The only difficulty faced by the governmental elites, in instigating their fully-protected subterranea-capital, was that the vast excavation projects calamitously unsettled the foundations of the corporate buildings above them, and many of those once-revered towers, such as The Shard and The Gherkin, finally toppled across the face of the city, in spectacular falls of screaming metal, crushing the final surface-level headquarters of the governmental elites with their remaining occupants.

The advance-guard of the Northern rebel brigades assessed the subterranean city, with unduped, wily eyes. Detachments were immediately dispatched back to the main body of rebels at Richmond, and returned after a few hours with huge suction tubes, which they inserted into the principal filtration apertures of the subterranea-city, to suck out all of its air; once the air was gone, the rebels abruptly reversed the direction of the generators powering the pumps, unleashing immense influxes of toxic chemicals transported from the North's now-obsolete plants, until the very last of those chemicals had been propelled, at maximum velocity, into the subterranea. Although a scattering of England's great elites were able to escape the subterranea – divining the rebels' plan and rapidly returning to the surface, before heading south towards Dover and south-westwards towards Dorset, where their remaining military forces were barracked – the remainder, lungs filled to bursting point with an amalgam of mutagen and sulphur, were lost. Soon, the bodies of hundreds of thousands of the asphyxiated governmental conscripts exited the subterranea, via the lost-rivers that ran into the Thames. The calamitous collapses within the over-excavated subterranea which had brought down London's corporate towers had also tilted the city's axis askew, so that the river now ran only in one direction, away from the sea. By nightfall, the mass of packed conscript-bodies had become so thick at Richmond, blocking the river's course entirely, that the main rebel forces were able to cross, as though stepping over logs.

The following dawn, the rebels' leader Iris, together with her adjutants, arrived at Bunhill Fields cemetery with the map of England's darkness, to execute the first of the four acts intended to eradicate England's myths, and cast it into oblivion as an entity. An immense, terminal silence had fallen over the entirety of London, now that its subterranean inhabitants had either been asphyxiated or were fleeing. Iris, dressed in her winter leather greatcoat, in expectation of summer storms, smiled upon that apocalypse. The Bunhill Fields dissenters' cemetery had been returned to a semi-flooded, pestilent terrain, as at its seventeenth-century origins. The gravestone of William Blake stood isolated from the other tombs, as though presciently displaced there to avert the future danger of the extraction of his bones by psychotic rebels, enraged by the wastelanding and fiery depopulation of the

North into envisioning the eradication of all of England's myths and traces, embodied in its four seminal figures. Although those rebels carefully pulverised the uprooted gravestone, rendering it into a material so fine that it sieved through their fingers like sand and poured to the waterlogged ground, the rebels had already established, through research in the surviving archives of London, that Blake's bones were not located directly beneath it, but close by, on the edge of a garden that had been transformed by the previous winter's incessant sleetfall into bitter ochre mud. The rebels dug down into that mud, which turned black and hard as they went deeper; after meticulous excavations among the centuries-old coffins, they unearthed the eroded, near-vanished bones of William Blake, collecting them into a jute sack which was slung over the shoulder of a sullen rebel boy.

In their explorations of the urban subterranea for any surviving conscripts still requiring culling, the rebels had soon discovered the immense reservoirs of petroleum, stored by the governmental elites of the South in reinforced tanks underneath the city's financial and corporate heart; two weeping rebel boys were assigned the task of igniting those tanks, once the main body of rebels had left the annulled megalopolis, on the next segment of their mapping of England's darkness. As the rebel brigades dispersed from Bunhill Fields and headed down towards the Thames, they discovered the first of long lines of sad-faced refugees who had deserted the urban subterranea before its contamination, or who had been arbitrarily barred from access to it by the governmental elites; those refugees were prepared now to crisscross what remained of England, in incessant transits, until they starved or else England ceased to exist, but they asked for mercy from the Northern rebels. The rebels, viewing them as London's cast-out detritus, magnanimously agreed to repopulate them along the far bank of the Thames, at a safe distance from London's oncoming conflagration, in and around the now-ruined Shepperton film-studios, so that the studio's hangars became the sole human settlement in the entire zonal wasteland of the depopulated London region, the refugees undertaking bare subsistence-farming, on a communal basis, around the derelict film-sets and between the abandoned, burnt-out motorway networks.

3

The rebel brigades streamed down towards the Thames, carrying their jute sack holding the bones of William Blake. The next stage of the mapping of England's darkness would be even more dangerous than the annulling of London's subterranea; the rebels had already heard that not all of the governmental, corporate and military elites had been eliminated (though all of the administrative elites had endured asphyxiation or crushing), and were regrouping with their still-sizeable forces in Dorset and Dover, determined to salvage England's great heritage of detritus, even at its far corners. For those surviving elites of the South, still unaware of the map of England's darkness that determined and drove the rebels' transits, those manoeuvres across England's face formed mysteries: mass-aberrations, to rank with the profound mystery of why the North had not allowed itself to be utterly subjugated, depopulated and wastelanded according to the retrenchment strategy devised to alleviate England's fall. At any stage of the mapping of England's darkness, the remaining governmental forces – many thousands of conscript phalanxes, along with several special units, so far held back from the conflict – could intervene to curtail the rebels' psychotic, punk-inspired project, and tear-apart that map.

The second axis-point on the charcoal-indented map – its traces still more blurred from the restless fingers of the rebels' leader, Iris, as she cursorily scanned it together with her adjutants, Lily and Patience, scratching with her fingernails at the emulsion of the photographic image on its reverse and striating the faces of the two dictators – was the village of Bladon, to the west. The rebels had decided to make their next journey by train, in contempt for all of the incessant walking which their uprising had so far entailed. By Tower Bridge, they commandeered a fleet of barges , intended by the govermental forces for the removal of accumulated debris from the excavated subterraneas beneath London's corporate towers, but then forgotten at the rebels' assault. The changed tidal flow hastened the barges' progress towards Waterloo station, and several barges overshot the adjacent landing-stage, their rebel cargoes never seen again. Many abandoned trains had been left at the station platforms, under the shattered glass canopy, and on the lines leading into the station, but the rebels still had to cram aboard. Every moment was an urgent one, in the execution of England's darkness. The battle-hallucinating rebel-drivers propelled the trains at speed, each positioned behind its predecessor.

Once the rebel trains had left London, the ignition of the petroleum reserves under the financial heart of the city could be initiated, and the weeping boys entrusted with that mission threw fiery torches through the apertures leading down into those reserves, the tanks' reinforced carapaces pre-cracked and leaking after being damaged by the calamitous fall of corporate towers; then, the weeping boys put their hands over their ears. The governmental administrators who had calculated the quantity of now-rare petroleum needed, in an emergency, to evacuate the elites of the South had vastly overestimated the required reserves, so the rebel boys fired an excess. A vertical column of vermilion flame rose into the summer sky above London, then spread outwards to engulf and raze the entire city, to the last ash. The detonation accompanying the incineration of the near-depopulated city (only a few urban die-hards had remained) was heard across Europe, but the intensity of the conflagration consumed even its own detonation, and within an hour, London had vanished, and a deep silence fell over that scorched-earth zone.

The Northern rebel brigades, on board their procession of trains, disregarded the sonic wave of London's conflagration. They experienced no triumph, and their mood grew more sombre as they entered England's heartland; they expected a concerted counterattack by the governmental forces that could overturn their enacting of the map of England's darkness, at any moment, and once isolated in England's heartland, the rebels were at their most vulnerable. The trains entered the nearest station to Bladon, each disgorging its content of rebels onto the platform before accelerating further up the line to allow the next train to unload. The lush terrain of forested lakes and colonnaded palaces that extended between the railway station and the village of Bladon presented a special challenge to the rebel brigades, in its transformation into irretrievably scorched and ashen wasteland – indistinguishable from London's former site – but they undertook that mission, under cooling bursts from summer storms.

The rebels met no resistance as they entered Bladon, their engineers carrying a vintage film-projector and a celluloid film-reel, ransacked from the same archives of London in which the exact location of Blake's bones had been determined. That film-reel constituted the sole looted material taken from London: all that was worth taking, and even then, only to heighten the rebels' envisioning of England's decimation; the engineers planned to erase the reel's images, immediately after their projection, and to break-down the projector into its constituent parts, dispersing them beyond all possibility of re-assembly.

The rebel brigades waited until the fall of night before they approached the tomb of Winston Churchill, set alongside the village's church. Each rebel carried a flaming torch that veered across the darkness. The gravestone held no text beyond Churchill's name and the dates of his birth and death, as though inscribed in the prescience that, at some point in the future, an amassing of Northern rebel factions, propelled beyond endurance into a lucid madness of terminal violence – after being subjugated to a campaign of arbitrary wastelanding and massacre – would seek to eliminate all traces and myths of England, embodied by its four seminal figures. With only a name, and two dates, that process of elimination was already near-annulled. The rebels stood aside as the film of Churchill's funeral procession, on 30 January 1965, through the avenues of London, was projected onto the facade of the church. The original spectators of the procession appeared stunned, and none wept; one hid his face from the film-camera with his hand, as though a criminal act was in progress now England's last moment had already lapsed, leaving behind only a maleficent debris, which it had then fallen, decades later, to the Northern rebels to clean away, as a lowly service-industry task, along with the bleached-out city of ghosts through which that funeral procession had passed.

As the rebels cracked-apart the graveslab and unearthed Churchill's bones, the soundtrack of the film, transmitted from a feedback-prone metal speaker placed beside the projector, blared out *Jerusalem*, and the brigades gathered around the cemetery first roared in fury as they heard Blake's hallucinated evocation of England, and howled with still greater anger on hearing of 'dark Satanic Mills', which instantly conjured for them the innumerable toxic chemical plants which had been positioned by the elites of the South at their cities' peripheries, but then calmed, on hearing of the great array of weaponry that Blake proposed, for a divine uprising which the rebels immediately appropriated, as their own.

Then, the decrepit film-projector malfunctioned, burst into flames, and consumed the images of Churchill's funeral along with the soundtrack's speaker, into an image-meltdown and a silencing. The rebels' torches were extinguished by the summer storm's final downpour, and darkness fell. The bones of Churchill were placed into a separate jute sack from those of Blake, and slung over the shoulder of a second sullen rebel boy.

At dawn, Iris stood shivering on the hill behind the Bladon cemetery, with its panorama out over the now-erased heartland of England, and again cursorily studied the map of England's darkness, a concentrated scowl on her face, along with her two adjutants, that group forming the lip-bitten punk-trinity of England's negation. She announced to the awakening rebels: 'We head south.'

4

In the event, the rebel brigades made an erratic movement south from Bladon, towards Moreton. The determining map of England's darkness held no detail on the gaps between the four axis-points to be erased by the rebels, its few annotations taking the form of exclaimed curses, or reflections on the status of the bones of England's four great 'rascals' that needed to be unearthed. The rebel brigades were guided by too-eager collaborators from the South who advised them to veer far to the west in order to elude ambushes from the Dorset-based conscript forces, with their superior knowledge of the terrain; but those rebels soon grew suspicious of their collaborator-guides, and in anger, selectively culled them according to the degree of their treachery. But none of the angry, dissident rebel-factions deserted the main body of the uprising, now the momentum for the final erasing of England was so strong. The rebels' leader, Iris, knew only that when the graveyards they traversed began to be filled with lichen-covered tombs of sea-captains, they would be nearing the coast. One dawn, the rebels approached Glastonbury Tor, and climbed to its summit, to look out through the mist at the waterway-striated flatlands around them, and re-orient themselves towards Dorset. Iris, walking barefoot, whispered to her adjutants: 'This is madness.' The region's entire population had fled to hide in caves, and all England had fallen into a deep silence. A beam of sunlight illuminated the Tor, and, after a moment's anguish, Iris grew certain of the rebels' imminent triumph, touching the Tor's earth and announcing that it would now be known, for all time, as Eddie Waring Tor.

Having re-oriented themselves from the Tor, the rebel brigades advanced southwards. The Dorset-based governmental forces bided their time beside the river Frome, amusing themselves by capturing then sodomising and decapitating the advance-guard of the rebels, sent ahead to ascertain the governmental forces' strength. Those conscripts now had nothing at all to lose, but in that extremity, were as certain of their imminent triumph as the rebels. Before long, the rebel factions would disintegrate into deadly in-fighting, the conscripts would pick off any survivors, and the North would be reclaimed, its wastelanding pursued to a just conclusion. Knowing that the entire uprising pivoted on the next battle, Iris established her late-summer headquarters in a former hospital for the criminally insane at the periphery of the village of East Coker. The hospital's century-old buildings had been categorised as obsolete decades earlier, and left to decay, so they had become submerged in foliage, undetectable to any governmental spies; forests grew from the roofs, the marble corridors echoed to the rebels' steps, and the high-ceilinged rooms still held the traces of medical experimentation undertaken on the insane. Iris began to strategise the coming confrontation with the governmental forces, while conducting deep reflections on the language which the North would adopt, once the language of England – terminally corrupted by subjugation, as the instrument through which all orders for the North's carbonising had been issued – had been annulled and cast into oblivion. Iris decided that in-depth research needed to be undertaken to document the deliriums of the 'Kings of the North' during their lives in lunatic asylums and hospitals for the criminally insane – Jimmy Savile, Peter Sutcliffe, Eddie Waring – in order to create a new language for the North, out of those glossolalia. One day, she entered the church of East Coker to gauge, by the density of tombs of sea-captains, how close to the coast the Northern uprising had reached. On one plaque, she saw the inscription: 'in my beginning is my end/in my end is my beginning'. Her adjutants asked: 'Shall we take the ashes from behind this plaque, to add them to the bones?' Iris shook her head: 'We already have all the ashes we need.'

In the hot days of England's last summer, the rebel brigades finally confronted the Dorset-based governmental forces, around the valley of the river Frome. Soon, both sides realised that their struggle had fallen into banality; however spectacular and frenzied the initial battles appeared, with astonishing acts of courage and self-sacrifice, and brutal massacres, they soon became mundane, for their participants. Elimination camps were set-up along the shallow river's banks, their human contents oscillating frequently between captured governmental conscripts and rebel fighters, at intervals of only a few hours, as the confrontation intensified. The just-slaughtered dead had to be urgently shovelled-out of the elimination camps, before new cullings could take place.

The conscript forces had become separated from their lines of communication, since most of the governmental elites commanding them had remained in Dover along with the special military units who would be deployed, as a last resort, to secure England's great heritage. As a result, in their abandonment, and once they had realised the banality of their imminent fall, those conscripts fought in disarray, often preferring to assassinate their own local commanders rather than engage the rebels, and finally proved gullible to Iris's strategy of luring them to the narrow wooden bridge over the river Frome at Moreton; trapped on that bridge and waiting in files to cross it, the end blurred with the beginning, they were nonchalantly obliterated in an adept pincer-movement of the rebel brigades, the final conscript culled at the bridge's exact centre.

On the river's far bank, the rebels discovered the grave of T.E. Lawrence, at the end of an annex to the village church's cemetery, as though placed there in the firm expectation, following Lawrence's death in a motorcycle crash on a military road nearby, that a horde of Northern rebels, intent on obliterating all of England's myths and its seminal, aberrant figures, would arrive, sooner or later, to appropriate his bones, and that act could be delayed, at least for a moment or two, by the subterfuge of his grave's isolated siting. The rebels knew nothing of Lawrence's wars, but had heard a more vital last-fragment of England's history, that his final journey, in February 1935, shortly before his motorcycle crash and week-long coma, had been by bicycle, from Bridlington, on the cold black Northern sea, down the spine of England, to Moreton; just before leaving Bridlington, he had been photographed (for the last time) on his bicycle, eyes looking down, leaning one hand against a brick wall which occupied the entire background of the image, the other on his left handlebar. The rebels spoke in hushed tones of that epic journey, which paralleled their own from the North, to that site. As a result, after meticulously hammering his gravestone to shards, they unearthed his bones in reverential silence, and placed them, over the shoulder of a third sullen rebel boy, in a third jute sack.

On the map of England's darkness, the site of Lawrence's minuscule cottage had been marked so violently, with a charcoal stroke that had pierced the paper on which it was inscribed (the rear exit-mark of that stroke, on the photograph of two dictators, emerged from the left eye of Pol Pot's eager interpreter), that it appeared, perversely, to hold all of England, as the pivotal objective of the Northern rebel brigades' uprising. The rebels walked back over the bridge, across a river of blood, and traversed the forest, past the site of Lawrence's death, to that blind-faced cottage, Clouds Hill, in a steep hollow. After spending several hours in Lawrence's study, in a profound dreaming, Iris decided to leave behind the map of England's darkness there, memorising its final stage before burying it in a tin box beside the cottage; that revelatory document of the rebels' mission would never fall into their adversaries' hands, in the event that they were all arbitrarily slaughtered, so close to their objective, in the conflict's last moment. But Iris was still certain of the triumph of England's imminent fall, and once a gasoline-soaked torch had been lit, at the fall of darkness, and Lawrence's cottage ignited, burning-up in an instant, to a blackened stone shell, England itself had been rendered into a beaten, sodomised and flagellated entity, ready for its final, offhand obliteration.

5

After their seizure of the bones of T.E. Lawrence, to add to those of Churchill and Blake, the rebel brigades advanced rapidly, with a final momentum, towards the last of the four axis–points – inscribed on their uprising's map of England's darkness, now securely interred beside the Clouds Hill site – that would allow them to eliminate all of England's awry myths, memory and history, embodied in its four aberrant 'rascals', and ensure that no renewed strategy, of England's elites, to depopulate and carbonise the North, could be formulated in the future. The distance from Moreton down to the coast was covered in a day, with the rebel brigades tracking fleeing survivors from the conflict by the Frome river bridge (conscripts too disabused even to have arrived in time for that massacre); finally, those conscripts were trapped, pinned-down with no escape, on the limestone shelf at Dancing Ledge, after scrambling down in desperation from the surrounding cliffs. A contingent of rebels was sent down to the ledge to slaughter them, before the glittering sea.

The Northern rebels continued unopposed along the coastal edge, aware that, at some point, they would be confronted by the last-surviving governmental forces, including its held-back special units; at the same time as they hurried to enact England's extinguishment (when they reached the Solent channel, the entire Goole faction was drowned in their impatience by attempting to swim across it, their bodies recovered and lined-up in rows on the floor of the Royal Victoria Hospital's military chapel), England's surviving forces were advancing to destroy them. Their numbers reduced, the rebel brigades circled Rye Bay, wading through the shallow sea so that they left no trace of their transit on the sun-illuminated white-sand dunes at Camber. The twin nuclear power plants up ahead, on the Dungeness headland, were both burning in the governmental forces' attempt to deter the rebels' advance via toxic contamination, but their long subjugation to chemical-plant toxins had already rendered the rebels totally impervious to whatever radiation those already-derelict plants could emit. All along the Dungeness shingle headland, the wooden fishermen's shacks were on fire, including the shack once occupied by England's last poet, Derek Jarman, so that it roared like Lawrence's cottage, in its vanishing. Hit by incendiary shells launched by governmental forces secreted along the coast, those shacks formed near-consumed balls of vermilion flames.

Their numbers reduced by the Solent catastrophe and now vulnerable to the governmental special units' imminent onslaught, the rebel brigades began to panic as they gazed over the Dungeness wasteland, multiple trails of vertical black smoke propelled from the burnt-out fisherman's shacks, as though each of those shacks embodied one of the carbonised cities of the North. It was impossible to know, when those special units would attack, and for the first time, the rebels had lost control of their uprising. But, after a rapid assessment of the terrain, Iris dispatched an advance-guard of engineers to the nearby Sound Mirrors at Greatstone, and the engineers attached stethoscopes to the listening-rods of those three vast, long-derelict warning devices, constructed in concrete at the end of the 1920s and designed to magnify and pinpoint all sonic traces that indicated an assault on England's coast, by its adversaries. The engineers positioned themselves directly beneath the Sound Mirrors, which they saw as mysterious terminal monuments to England's disintegration, listening intently; soon, the reverberations of the concave mirrors, transmitted through their listening-rods, warned the engineers that the governmental special units were approaching the Greatstone gravel lakes. Iris had just enough time to instruct the most fearsome rebel brigades to encircle those units from behind, via the abandoned tarmac runways of the Lydd airfield, them charge them from the rear (the 'sodomy tactic', as Iris's adjutants called it) and from both sides, so that they were propelled into the deep, aquamarine waters of the Greatstone gravel pits, beside the Sound Mirrors, and all drowned, mercilessly beaten-back by the rebels as they tried to reach the shores, their cries infinitely magnified by the mirrors, out over the coast to Europe's lands, in a final lamentation, of England's ending.

The remaining governmental, corporate and military elites of England had accompanied their special units from Dover, certain of victory, and were rapidly rounded-up by the rebels as they attempted to burrow themselves into holes in the shingle. They immediately announced that they wanted to negotiate, and were willing to accept an arrangement by which the South became a vassal colony of the North, ready for any subjugation, on condition that its surviving elites were permitted to retain their power, and preserve, too, any remaining detritus of England's heritage, in the expectation that, in some century of the distant future, it could be reactivated, and a new England conjured. The elites were then noosed, cursing, to a long, unsteady scaffold of driftwood on the Greatstone shingle, a wooden crate or stool under each set of feet, then the crates and stools were nonchalantly kicked-away by the rebel executioners, and the elites of England all hanged.

Leaving England's elites swinging in the summer-scented coastal breeze, the rebels moved on, an hour to the north, to the last of the four axis-points inscribed on the map of England's darkness. In the cemetery of the twelfth-century Old Romney church, they shattered to shards the upright slab of Derek Jarman's gravestone, marked solely with his name, as though no other inscription were viable. Jarman, entombed with his 'controversialist' regalia, as the final saint and anti-saint of England, and its terminal poet, had been a source of intense passion to the punk-rock instigators of the Northern uprising, and though those instigators had already been entirely culled in factional in-fighting – through what the surviving rebels evoked as 'massacre games' – a trace of his memory had been transmitted to those instigators' descendants, including their leader, Iris, eroded to a fragile echo, only a hair's-breadth from oblivion, but still present, so that the rebels handled his bones lovingly, in their desecration of England. The bones were consigned to a fourth jute sack, carried over the shoulder of the most sullen, shock-haired rebel boy of all.

The rebels returned across the shingle to the Dungeness headland. Their work was almost done. All that now remained, was to ritually eradicate England – according to a cryptic, half-effaced annotation inscribed in charcoal on the map of England's darkness – through the irreparable mixing-together into one jute sack of the bones of its four great 'rascals', Blake, Churchill, Lawrence and Jarman, and the jettisoning of that amalgam of bones into the sea. The sullen boys with the jute sacks disputed whose sack the remainder of the bones should be poured-into, beating one another's lips swollen, but Iris hissed to silence them and arbitrated, pointing to Lawrence's sack. Once the shattered bones – broken again and again, on the rebels' transits of England – had been mixed, Iris herself took the sack and climbed to a high shingle ridge above the edge of the sea, then hurled the sack in an arc, so that the bones and ash-fragments were propelled outwards, hitting the surface of the sea in a scattered sequence of momentary impacts, as though writing their own inscription, of England's fall. One skull appeared to be supported by the sea's surface, before sinking down, too. Iris turned back towards the rebels gathered behind her, weeping in exultation.

Night fell over the Dungeness headland, in an all-engulfing silence, on the last day of England's final summer, all trace of that land now voided and forgotten (except for the memories embedded in this record), as the Northern rebels looked out over the sea one last time, away towards Europe, and then turned, towards all of the devastated, scorched-earth wasteland-terrains that had to be traversed, as they returned, in their factions, to the North, to begin again.

One Execration, Two Lamentations

1

now we'll execrate England, one last time
and recount what we have accomplished
– we, the punk-inspired rebel factions –
in our eradication of England:
by eradicating England,
we created, too, an inspirational darkness:
an inspiration to Europe

we were ready to continue our onrush,
to cross the Channel from Dungeness
to decimate Europe, too,
if we had not been certain,
that the viral example of our act of oblivion
– our uprising from the void, to the void –
would irresistibly consume Europe too,
as it now has...

once the civil war was over,
our rebel factions returned to the North
and never returned to the South
that once-time excursion was enough,
as in the era, long ago, when our children
were taken to the South, by train,
to be shown its horrors

and then returned safely to the North, by night's fall,

or during other, long-forgotten, eras of warfare,

when the inhabitants of the North

found themselves conscripted into England's armies

and were shipped to its colonies

– Palestine, Iraq –

or to its killing zones

– Gallipoli, El Alamein –

traversing, on the way to the Thames troop-ship ports

the brutal corporate heart of England,

so that they yearned, without exception,

for the devil's ground of the North

and execrated England,

for dispossessing them of their youth and their blood

all of the great hotels of the Northern cities

had been damaged in the uprising

– the Purbeck-marble facades pitted by rocket-fire,

the roofs' viewing-balconies transformed into helicopter-pads,

the ballrooms' chandeliers shattered or wrenched-out,

the turkish baths in the basements graffitied by doomed conscripts,

the suites reeking of the governmental commanders' fear-sweat of defeat,

and blood everywhere –

so our first task, even before clearing away the chemical-plant debris,

was to restore those ruined hotels to their glory

– venerating the suites inhabited by the demented Kings of the

North,

above all, Jimmy Savile, Eddie Waring –

and to instil them with the nihilistic power conjured by our victory

in a boarded-up suite of the Queen's Hotel, Leeds

– sealed when its last occupant, Eddie Waring,

emitting unstoppable torrents of delirious glossolalia,

was transported to the High Royds psychiatric hospital –

we discovered an archive of books and documents:

the final books surviving,

after the incineration of all paper-based media

and their transferral to digital data,

before England's crash, and that data's crash

and so we finally learned about the great uprisings of the North

only after we had executed our own

and we learned of England's history of beauty and corruption

only after we had erased it, by retributive instinct

– we read and memorised the Preface to *Milton*

we read and memorised *A History of the English-Speaking Peoples*

we read and memorised *Seven Pillars of Wisdom*

we read and memorised *Dancing Ledge* –

and we retained one word, naming our uprising forever a 'triumph',

from Lawrence's subtitle to *Seven Pillars of Wisdom*...

then, to extirpate England still more completely from all memory,

we forgot all trace of those books,

consigned them to the ashes rendered from all that was England,

placed those ashes in a box

and returned it to that boarded-up suite at the Queen's Hotel,

where it remains to this day...

now our life is banal

after the adventure of our uprising,

so banal,

that we may all kill one another one day

– we, the triumphant rebel factions –

in our land of riches

our uprising's leader, Iris, vanished without trace

on the journey from Dungeness, back to the North,

her vanishing so total

that we believe she must still live

– a hidden recluse, under the assumed name Amalasumtha,

with her adjutants, Patience and Lily –

ready to save us again,

if the North must ever rise again

now we rule over our mundane Northern void

from the roof-terraces,

from the state-rooms,

from the subterranean turkish-baths,

of the Queen's Hotel, Leeds, and the Grand Hotel, Scarborough

and from the sites of our four Northern parliaments

which we built in cementless granite blocks

on the high moor

– Muker, Hardraw Scar, Low Row, Stalling Busk:

four sites, to negate the four mythic axis-points of the South's

power –

and inhabited for an instant

until our own power proved intolerable to us,

so we dismantled and demolished them

and now we look out from their ruins

from the high moor pinnacle,

above the Hardraw Scar waterfall,

our eyes transit from one coast to another:

from the North-West terrain, so devastated

by the all-out massacre-games

waged between the Manchester and Liverpool rebel-factions

that it could never be repopulated

and will remain a scorched-earth wasteland, to the end of time...

across the snapped aluminium chimneys

of the Pennine cities' chemical plants

and the great domed mausoleum

– styled, in Istrian stone, on that of Theodoric –

of the Yorkshire Ripper,

his body transported back from the cemetery-grounds

of the Broadmoor hospital for the criminally insane,

where our uprising's instigator

– hallucinating in a derelict pornographic cinema –

once envisioned him in profound dialogue

with that other King of the North, Jimmy Savile

and, finally, our eyes gaze across

to the North-Eastern coasts

of the cold black Northern seas

into which great ochre estuaries and rivers still flow

the water tainted still,

by the blood of the sailors and trawler-crews

mercilessly massacred by conscript phalanxes,

in our glorious era of denudation

now,

our rich land of the North

is nothing

mundane and emptied

but we do what we like, here,

and we can conjure anything we want

from our void

at any instant,

once we abandon our final, compulsive execration of England

all our lamentations now are for:

the children of the Northern cities: all dead, all dead

our walls, facades, hoardings, screens: all gone, all gone

our elations, passions, frenzies, deliriums: all burned-up, all burned-up

our killing-grounds, death-camps, cinemas, asylums: all emptied, all emptied...

but we lament, too:

that what vanished, of England,

may now endure in obsession, ineradicable

– and thereby infiltrate our lamentation,

so that we speak it in the language of our former subjugation,

the language of our wastelanding, of our near-eradication:

the language of England,

which will be silenced,

at this lamentation's end

through the institution of a new language,

of Northern delirium, of punk-rock lineage –

so we lament England's ineradicability

in these fragments' traces

that form a *Jerusalem*-spear of burning, carbonised gold,

stuck into our eyes

– these fragments' memories, lacerating our skins –

but, when these last fragments are gone

expelled from our devils' eyes

expelled from our devils' tongues

expelled from our devils' ears

expelled from our devils' pages,

then England, too, is gone